Dr. Ernest Drake's

Dragonology™

Pocket Adventures

The
Winged Serpent

Edited by

Dugald A. Steer, B.A. (Brist), S.A.S.D.

Ernest Drake

THE TEMPLAR COMPANY:

Publishers of rare & unusual books.

[ALL RIGHTS RESERVED.]

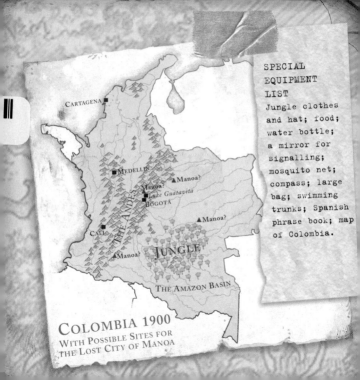

SPECIAL
EQUIPMENT
LIST
Jungle clothes
and hat; food;
water bottle;
a mirror for
signalling;
mosquito net;
compass; large
bag; swimming
trunks; Spanish
phrase book; map
of Colombia.

CARTAGENA

MEDELLIN

Manoa?

Manoa?
Lake Guatavita
BOGOTÁ

THE ANDES

Manoa?

CALI

Manoa?

JUNGLE

THE AMAZON BASIN

COLOMBIA 1900
WITH POSSIBLE SITES FOR
THE LOST CITY OF MANOA

Welcome to Dr. Drake's
WINGED SERPENT ADVENTURE.

The year is 1900. A huge serpent
has been disturbed in the lake
where it lives near Bogotá in
Colombia. It is said that this lake
is the actual site of the fabled *El
Dorado*. Are you skilled enough
to tackle the challenges of Dr.
Drake's Colombian adventure?

The Secret and Ancient Society of Dragonologists
DRAGONOLOGICAL MISSION

Date: 13th May 1900   Location: Bogotá, Colombia
Mission: A savage serpent has been disturbed by treasure-hunters
diving in its lake home. In order to find and return the
stolen treasure you will need to find the lost Chibcha city
of Manoa and seek the assistance of its dragon guardian.

When you arrive in Bogotá, high in the Andes, Señor Hada, the Colombian representative of the S.A.S.D. shows you a picture in the museum. "That, amigo, is *El Dorado*—the Gilded One," he explains. "He was a great king. Every year his servants would blow gold dust over him and he would dive into Lake Guatavita in order to befriend the serpent there. It is said that he lived in a city full of gold, called Manoa. That city has been lost for a long time, but now you must find it so you can return the stolen treasure." It is time for you to make a decision. Do you:

A. Begin at the treasure-hunters' camp. [go to **7**]

B. Begin at Lake Guatavita. [go to **11**]

2 Downstream you find some rocks. Although they are slippery, you start out, and halfway you notice the water is full of hungry piranhas. Luckily you manage not to slip and return to the old bridge where you see that there is indeed the remains of an ancient trail, marked by carved rocks. You set out along the trail. [go to **17**]

3 You climb down to the lakeside. Perhaps you can befriend the serpent, and learn more about the artefacts that have gone missing? But you do not have time to ask. A huge tail slithers out of the water like an enormous tentacle, wraps itself around your legs and begins to pull you deep down into the lake, until you are...

DRAGGED TO A WATERY DOOM!

4 When you get to Lake Guatavita, the dragon is waiting. "I defeated the wyvern but I did not kill him," he explains. "But by the time he recovers the charm will have worn off." Now you must take back the treasure. Do you:

A. Accept the dragon's aid and raid the camp. [go to **9**]

B. Raid the camp on your own. [go to **34**]

5 After the dragon has passed by, you resume your climb. At the top are a mighty pair of stone gateposts. You have reached Manoa! You are not the first, because there is a blackened skeleton, still wearing a rusting helmet, just outside the gate. It seems to be clutching a bag. Do you:
A. Examine the skeleton carefully. [go to **13**]
B. Get into the city and under cover. [go to **21**]

6 Unfortunately, you are only half-way across the bridge when you hear a cracking sound. You start to run, but the ropes of the bridge snap, throwing you into the boiling river. You have landed right in the middle of a huge shoal of man-eating piranhas, and in seconds you are...

DEVOURED BY RAVENOUS FISH!

7 Lake Guatavita is not far from Bogotá, and the treasure hunters' camp is near the lake. When you arrive, you are met by a tall man who asks you your business. Do you:

A. Say you are a tourist and leave. [go to **16**]

B. Warn him that he is in great danger, because of the artefacts his team have taken. [go to **24**]

8 The Chibchas are taking no chances. They are here to protect the secrets of their hidden city at all costs. Before you can even open your Spanish phrase book, they fire off a volley of arrows at you. These arrows are specially prepared using deadly venom from the posion-dart frog, and before you can shout *¡Amigo!* you are...

SLAUGHTERED IN A HAIL OF ARROWS!

9 The mere appearance of the dragon scares all of the treasure-hunters away except for the dark dragonologist. But he seems to have used up all of his dragondust charming the wyvern, and so you are soon in possession of the stolen artefacts. Now you are ready to go to the lake. [go to **38**]

10 After you have pulled down quite a lot of foliage you find a narrow window that you can just squeeze through. You find yourself inside some kind of temple room with a large tub in the centre. But just as you are about to investigate further, you hear a roar outside. Do you:

A. Decide to talk to the angry dragon. [go to **22**]

B. Leap into the tub to hide. [go to **37**]

11 You arrive at Lake Guatavita. Clearly it is the site of an extinct volcano, because the lake is perfectly round and surrounded on all side by cliffs. You seem to see movement in the otherwise still waters. Do you:

A. Go and take a closer look. [go to **3**]

B. Survey the area from high ground. [go to **16**]

12 You reach the old rope bridge and go down the river to cross over using the rocks. On the other side you can see what seem to be people hiding among the trees keeping a watchful eye on the bridge. Do you:

A. Sneak past them without finding out if they are the dragon's Chibcha friends. [go to **4**]

B. Call, "I am a friend! I come in peace." [go to **8**]

13 The clothes the skeleton is wearing seem so old that it might even have been here since the days of the Conquistadores! In the bag you find two gold coins, a book that turns to dust in your hands as you open it, a gold chain with "Maria" engraved on it, and a vellum scroll. At the top of the scroll you see the word "Manoa". →

There is a Spanish message on the scroll. Luckily, you have brought a Spanish phrase book.

𝕸anoa

En busca de mi oro
no entre por la puerta.
Allí espera la muerte,
pero no en la huerta.

allí – there;   *busca* – search;   *de* – of;   *en* – in;
espera – waits;   *huerta* – orchard   *la* – the;   *mi* – my;
muerte – death;   *no entre* – do not enter;   *oro* – gold;
pero no – but not;   *por* – by;   *puerta* – door

¡Caramba! Do you:

A. Avoid the door in the courtyard. [go to **21**]

B. Go through the door very carefully. [go to **28**]

14 After three hours, you cannot climb very quickly, but you do your best! Unfortunately, your best is not good enough. In next to no time the enormous dragon has swept down upon you and, without giving you any chance to explain yourself, it lets out a mighty squawk and you are...

BLASTED WITH A JET OF FLAME!

15 This was the right choice! Far above you, you see a huge wyvern appear and attack the guardian amphithere. It must be the charmed one. You can only hope the amphithere wins. Meanwhile you must get back to Lake Guatavita with a supply of gold dust. Do you:

A. Return the same way you came. [go to **12**]

B. Take a new route, just in case. [go to **32**]

16 You decide to get a high viewpoint and climb to the top of a tall peak called Cerro de Montserrat. As you gaze across the mountains, you wonder how you will ever be able to find Manoa, when so many have failed. Do you:

A. Decide to steal back the treasure. [go to **27**]

B. Set off down into the jungle. [go to **33**]

17 The old trail eventually heads back up into the mountains. There, you see some steps have been carved out of the rock. There must be thousands of them, all heading upwards. You have nearly reached Manoa. Do you:

A. Climb up the mountain, but avoid the steps in case the dragon is guarding them. [go to **23**]

B. Head on up the steps. [go to **29**]

18 You leave, and the man does not follow. You cannot decide what to do. You would prefer that the dragon did not destroy these people, no matter how bad they have been. Do you:

A. Decide to enlist the dragon's aid, but tell the dragon to spare them. [go to **9**]

B. Go back and talk to the man. [go to **24**]

19 Running from the camp, you did not reckon on meeting a huge, feathery dragon of the type known as an amphithere! You realise too late that this must be the guardian dragon of Manoa. He has been seeking the treasure, too! "Thief!" he roars, as he coils his huge tail around you and...

SQUEEZES THE LIFE OUT OF YOU!

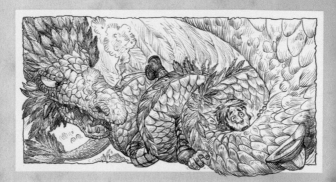

20 "I know Dr. Drake," says the dragon. "If you have come to return stolen treasure, I will help you. But you must know the treasure hunters have a dragon of their own. One is a dark dragonologist who has brought a charmed wyvern to attack me!"

A. Go out the door to the courtyard. [go to **28**]

B. Climb through the window again. [go to **35**]

21 You search and find a small passage to the side of a courtyard that leads to the ruins of what may have been some kind of orchard. But although you look you cannot see any way into the building that backs onto the courtyard. Do you:

A. Begin to pull down the foliage that has grown up, keeping a lookout for spiders. [go to **10**]

B. Carefully cross the courtyard. [go to **28**]

22 The angry guardian dragon is making a terrible commotion, but you begin to relax as you realise that it cannot possibly get in through the small window. Now is your chance to explain your mission to the dragon, and hope that it will help you. "I was sent here by Dr. Drake of the Secret and Ancient Society of Dragonologists," you shout. "He is a friend to dragons." [go to **20**]

23 Climbing the mountain is not too difficult at first, but it is not long before you get stuck. You have not brought climbing equipment, and you find yourself in a series of gulleys that always end in overhanging cliffs. It seems as though the people who built Manoa found the only route up the mountain after all. [go to **29**]

24 The man laughs, and shows you the artefacts. "You say they are cursed, señor?" he says. "I do not think so!" But you think so. Seeing your chance, you grab the artefacts and start to run. But it is not good. The tall man must be an athlete! He catches up with you on a cliff overlooking the lake and with a push...

THROWS YOU TO YOUR DOOM!

25 You climb up a new peak, and look around. There is no sign of a lost city, but as you look back towards Cerro de Montserrat you think you can see someone on the top. You signal with your mirror and the person begins waving two flags. It is a message in semaphore, a way of signalling using flags! The first message tells you the person is Señor Hada, and that he has discovered new information about Manoa. The second message is:

SEMAPHORE.

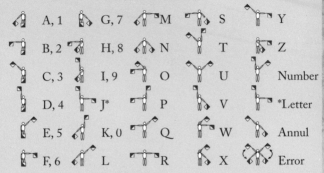

A, 1   G, 7   M   S   Y

B, 2   H, 8   N   T   Z

C, 3   I, 9   O   U   Number

D, 4   J*   P   V   *Letter

E, 5   K, 0   Q   W   Annul

F, 6   L   R   X   Error

Finally you have the clue that will help you find the lost city! Wave your arms to signal "thank you," and then decide what you are going to do:

A. Go ten miles west. [go to **32**]

B. Go ten miles north. [go to **36**]

26 You begin by keeping to the mountains, but you are worried that, without any clues, it might take you a long time to find Manoa, and your provisions might not last. Do you:

A. Return to the camp, after all, in order to steal back the treasure. [go to **31**]

B. Keep on, heading into the jungle. [go to **33**]

27 You wait until nightfall, and then creep quietly to the treasure-hunter's camp that lies not far from Lake Guatavita. You are not sure if they will still keep any of the treasure which they have found here, until you see a tent which looks extremely well guarded. Do you:

A. Leave, and search for Manoa. [go to **26**]

B. Wait for an opportunity. [go to **31**]

28 Although you are very careful to look out for traps as you cross the courtyard, you step on a loose tile. There is a loud click and then two gigantic spiked meshes swing down on you. Despite your suspicious mind you can't go on and you can't walk out. You're caught in a trap, and...

IMPALED ON SHARP SPIKES!

29 You were right to worry about the guardian dragon watching the steps. You have climbed for about three hours, when you see a large black shape flapping towards you from the top of the mountain. It looks like an amphithere. Do you:

A. Hide in a gulley, covered with stones. [go to **5**]

B. Keep going as quickly as possible. [go to **14**]

30 The ride begins in style as you swoop over the mountains. But then you see another dragon flying towards you. It is the charmed wyvern! Normally it would not even be here, far less attack an amphithere, but now it has no choice. And as the scaly beasts begin to battle, twisting and biting in the air, you are soon...

A VICTIM OF A DRAGON FIGHT!

31 It isn't long before you have a chance to take the treasure. One of the guards has to anwer the call of nature, while the other has fallen asleep! You creep inside the tent, and find a chest that contains ancient gold items. You place them in your bag. Now all you have to do is return them to the lake, and the serpent will be happy. [go to **19**]

32 You head into the jungle, for ten, twenty, thirty miles, and quickly get lost. You are excited to find a small collection of artefacts: it must mean you cannot be too far off course! You try to retrace your steps but your compass seems to be broken, and you soon find yourself going round and round in circles. Days pass until you are...

LOST FOREVER IN THE JUNGLE!

33 You set off down into the jungle, but soon find yourself lost as there are very few paths to follow, and you have no idea which way you should be going. To your left lie the mountains; to your right, thousands of miles of forest. Do you:

B. Return to the treasure-hunters' camp, and warn the tall man about the gold artefacts. [go to **24**]

A. Climb back up the mountains again. [go to **25**]

34 Deciding it will be safer if you raid the treasure-hunters' camp on your own, you wait until nightfall to make your approach. You are very quiet, but just as you are about to enter the camp, a tall man steps out of the shadows. You realise this is the dark dragonologist, a man who uses the knowledge of dragons for his own ends, and who cares nothing at all for their conservation or protection. Do you:

A. Say that you are lost and leave. [go to **18**]

B. Demand to see the artefacts. [go to **24**]

35 Outside you meet the dragon, a magnificent winged serpent. "I have lived here a long time," explains the dragon. "My forefathers owed a favour to the Chibcha Indians, and when the Conquistadores arrived, stealing all their gold, the Indians decided to hide what they had here in the city of Manoa. We have been protecting it ever since. But we must go to Lake Guatavita without delay. You may ride me, if you like." Do you:

A. Decide that you will return on foot. [go to **15**]

B. Accept the dragon's offer. [go to **30**]

36 Using your compass, you head north. The route takes you back down into the jungle again, but you are very careful not to lose your way. Soon you come to a rickety rope bridge strung across a river. It looks dangerous, but it is a promising sign because it means there must be some kind of trail here! You have a choice to make. Do you:

A. Avoid the bridge, and walk down the river, looking for another crossing place. [go to **2**]

B. Get across the bridge quickly. [go to **6**]

37 As soon as you leap into the tub you find that it is not a tub at all, but a rather deep vat. Also, instead of ordinary water, it contains nothing but pure, fine gold dust. You realise this must be where the gold dust was stored that was used to cover *El Dorado* before he went swimming in Lake Guatavita. The problem is that the dust is so fine it acts in almost exactly the same way as sinking sand. And the more you struggle to get out, the more you sink, until at last...

YOU DROWN IN A VAT OF GOLD!

38 At the lake you put on your swimming trunks, and get ready to return the stolen objects. First, you cover yourself in gold dust, and then, taking the objects in your hands, dive into the lake. The serpent rises to receive them and then slips back into the deep waters. As you are finally about to go home you are treated to a magnificent sight—both the lake serpent and the guardian dragon of Manoa, flying and swimming over Lake Guatavita, in a grateful salute.

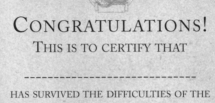

Congratulations!

This is to certify that

HAS SURVIVED THE DIFFICULTIES OF THE
WINGED SERPENT ADVENTURE.
YOU HAVE SUCCEEDED ADMIRABLY!
DR. DRAKE
IS PROUD OF YOUR
DRAGONOLOGICAL ACHIEVEMENT!!

Ernest Drake